For
Sam, Peb, Trish and Ben.
With all my love, El.

Scholastic Children's Books
Commonwealth House, 1-19 New Oxford Street
London WC1A 1NU, UK
a division of Scholastic Ltd
London ~ New York ~ Toronto ~ Sydney ~ Auckland
Mexico City ~ New Delhi ~ Hong Kong

First published in paperback in the UK by Scholastic Ltd, 2005

Copyright © Ella Burfoot, 2005

ISBN 0 439 96844 5

All rights reserved

Printed in Singapore

2 4 6 8 10 9 7 5 3 1

Louie
and the
Monsters

Ella Burfoot

Louie didn't
like monsters,

but monsters
liked Louie.

They followed him up the stairs . . .

. . . and all the way back down again.

They sat at the table and ate his dinner,
and got the peas stuck in their teeth.

They played silly games and broke his toys,
and drew on the wall with his favourite pens.

They squeezed themselves into Louie's den, and there was no more room for Louie.

They dribbled and drooled . . .

and burped out loud!

Louie had had enough.
He shouted and screamed and jumped up
and down, and the monsters left the house
without a sound.

Then Louie climbed the stairs alone,

and ate his dinner on his own.

And he sat in his den all by himself.
But the stairs were boring and
he hated peas . . . and his den was too big
with no one but him.

Monsters weren't really so bad.
Louie wished that he hadn't been
mean and shouted and screamed.
He wished most of all that
they would come back.

He took some paper and his
favourite pens, and drew some
letters to make a word.

He took the word and a piece of tape,

and went and stuck it on the gate.

Then he went back to the house
and upstairs to his room.

SU

Monsters liked Louie . . .

. . . but Louie
LOVED monsters!

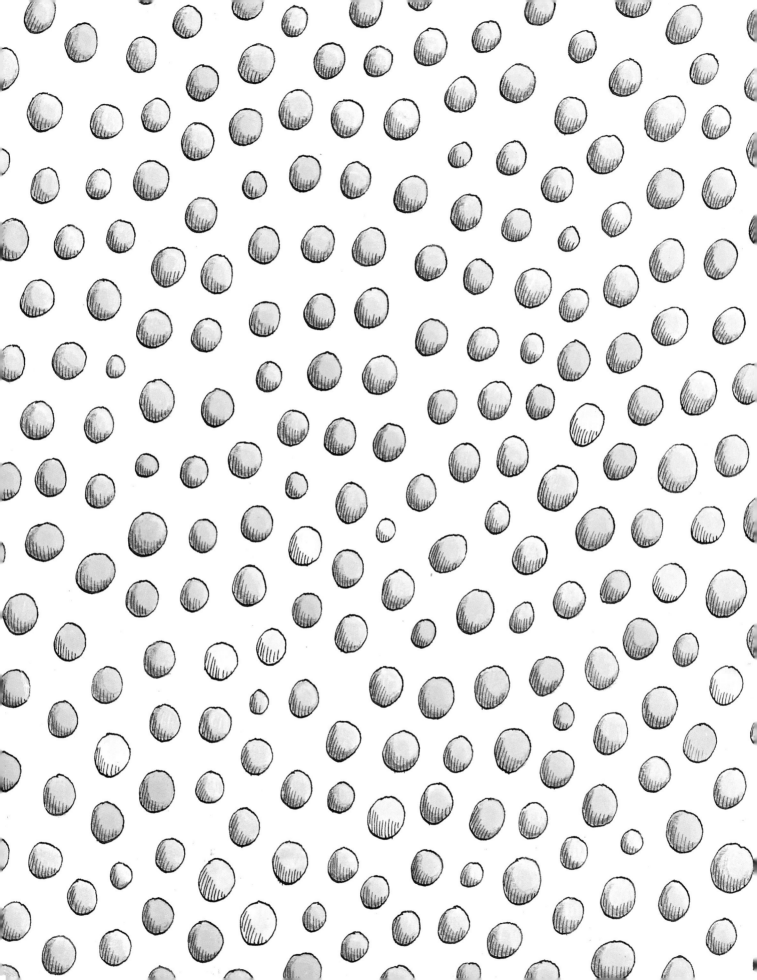